MAYWOOD PUBLIC LIBRARY
3 1312 0010
W9-BUH-399

by James Marshall

DIAL BOOKS FOR YOUNG READERS · NEW YORK

For my sister, Cynthia

Published by
Dial Books for Young Readers
A Division of Penguin Books USA Inc.
375 Hudson Street
New York, New York 10014

Printed in Hong Kong by
South China Printing Company (1988) Limited

Library of Congress Cataloging in Publication Data
Marshall, James, 1942– Fox outfoxed
by James Marshall. — 1st ed.
p. cm.
Summary: Fox competes in a big race, gives away his comic books,
and goes trick-or-treating on Halloween with his friends.
ISBN 0-8037-1036-4. ISBN 0-8037-1037-2 (lib. bdg.)
[1. Foxes — Fiction.] I. Title.
PZ7.M35672Fs 1992 [E]—dc20 91-21815 CIP AC

First Edition
3 5 7 9 10 8 6 4 2

The art for each picture consists of an ink, pencil,
and watercolor painting, which is scanner-separated
and reproduced in full color.

Reading Level 1.9

A FASTER FOX

Carmen's
Baby

One Saturday morning
Fox went out for some fun.
At Carmen's house
something was up.
"The Big Race is today,"
said Carmen.
Fox looked at Carmen's race car.
"Does it have an engine?" he said.
"It has pedals," said Carmen.
"That's no fun," said Fox.
"First prize in The Big Race
is a free shopping spree
at the candy store," said Carmen.

Fox ran home to build
his own race car.
"There isn't much time," he said.
"May I help?" asked Louise.
"Go away," said Fox.

Then Fox had one of his great ideas.

He ran after Louise.

"You can help," said Fox.

"But you must do as I say."

"Oh goody!" said Louise.

Fox made it to the starting line
just in the nick of time.
He looked smug.

"On your mark!" cried the starter.

"Get set! Go!"

The race was on!

Fox shot ahead of the others.

He was really moving!

He crossed the finish line.

But he kept right on going...

smack into Mrs. O'Hara's
pretty flower garden.
"*You!*" said Mrs. O'Hara.
"It wasn't my fault!"
said Fox.

Suddenly out popped Louise.

"Did I run fast enough, Fox?"

she said.

"Aha!" yelled the starter.

"Shame, shame!" cried the others.

Fox spent the rest of the day
working in Mrs. O'Hara's garden.
"I hope you learned your lesson,"
said Dexter.
But Fox was in no mood to hear *that.*

COMIC FOX

COMING SOON !!! CREEPY TALES
FRAKEN FOX

Fox had lots and lots
of comic books.
"Are you sure you have enough?"
said Mom.
"I could always use more,"
said Fox.
"I wasn't serious," said Mom.
"I couldn't live without my comics,"
said Fox.
And he took his ten best comics
to read in the yard.

"This is great," said Fox.

Just then his pretty new neighbor

Lulu came by.

"May I see?" she said.

"Sure," said Fox.

“You don’t read *comics*!” said Lulu.

“They’re for little kids.”

“Er... they’re not mine,” said Fox.

“I just found them.

I was about to throw them away.”

"Then you won't mind if I take them for my little brother," said Lulu.

"Er...," said Fox.

"Bye-bye," said Lulu.

And she was gone.

"My ten best comics!" cried Fox.

He felt sick all afternoon.

Later he went for a walk.

In front of Lulu's house

he couldn't believe his eyes.

1043

Lulu was reading Fox's comics
out loud to her friends.
"These are great!"
said her friends.
"Wait until you hear *this* one!"
said Lulu.
"It's my favorite!"
"Where did you get these?"
said her friends.
"Oh," said Lulu,
"I was *very* clever."

Fox had to go home and lie down.

"Is he dying?" said Louise.

"No," said Mom.

"But he's taking it pretty hard."

FOX OUTFOXED

Halloween was coming up.

Fox and the gang were excited.

"My costume will be really wild!"

said Carmen.

"Think of all the tricks we can pull,"

said Dexter.

"Keep your voices down,"

whispered Fox.

"We don't want any little kids

tagging along."

On Halloween Fox was ready.
He had worked hard on his costume.
"No one will ever know me," he said.
"Fox, dear," said Mom,
"Louise is all set
to go trick-or-treating."
"You're not serious!" said Fox.
"She'll just get in the way,
and her costume is *dumb*!"
"You're so mean," said Mom.

Carmen and Dexter were waiting.

"Mom made me bring Louise," said Fox.

"Little kids are trouble," said Dexter.

"I'll handle this," said Carmen.

"Now see here!" she said to Louise.

"Tonight I have magic powers.

Do not cause any problems.

Or I'll turn you into a *real* pumpkin!"

Louise didn't say a word.

"Little kids will believe *anything,*"

whispered Carmen to Fox.

They set off trick-or-treating.

Soon Dexter had an ugly thought.

"Little kids always get

the most treats," he said,

"and there won't be enough for us."

"Hmm," said Carmen.

At the corner of Cedar and Oak

they put Louise on a bench.

"Now don't you move," said Fox.

"We'll be right back."

And Louise was left all alone.

Fox and the gang went
to Mrs. O'Hara's house.
"Trick or treat!" they called out.
"Hello, Fox," said Mrs. O'Hara.
"I'd know *you* anywhere.
But where is your little sister?"
"Oh, she's around," said Fox.

Fox and the gang
went on trick-or-treating
until their bags were full.
"Let's go get Louise," said Fox.
They went back to the bench.
"Come on, Louise," said Fox.
But Louise didn't move.
"Come on, Louise!"
said Dexter and Carmen.
But Louise didn't budge.
"Oh my gosh!" cried Fox.
"It's a *real* pumpkin!"
"Wow!" said Carmen.

WANTED
RAT FACE

They went to the cops.

"My little sister got turned into
a pumpkin!" cried Fox.
"But it wasn't my fault!"
"Well, well," said Officer Bob.
"Maybe we could bake a nice pie."
"This is serious!" cried Fox.
"*Do* something!"
"I'm afraid it's too late,"
said Officer Bob.
Fox and the gang
left the police station.

On the way home

Fox tripped on his costume.

"Look out!" cried Carmen.

Fox went flying.

The pumpkin landed with a splat.

"Now you've done it!" said Dexter.

"Poor Louise," said Carmen.

"What a mess."

Fox put the pieces into a shopping bag and ran to the hospital.

"Put Louise back together!" he cried.

"*Really*, Fox!" said Nurse Wendy.
"I don't have time for your jokes.
I've got a lot of sick people here."

Fox went home.

"Sit down, Mom," he said.

And he told her about Louise.

"That *is* too bad," said Mom.

"You're not cross?" said Fox.

"These things happen," said Mom.

"And we don't really *need* Louise."

"Don't say that!" cried Fox.

"She was always in the way," said Mom.

"Not always," said Fox.

"Would you be sweet to Louise

if we had her back?" said Mom.

"Oh, *yes*!" said Fox.

"I would even let her read my comics."

Louise flew out of the closet.

"Tra la!" she sang.

Fox nearly fainted.

"I get to read your comics!"

said Louise.

Later Fox heard Mom and Louise talking.

"Fox really thought I turned into a pumpkin!" said Louise.

"Big kids will believe *anything*!"

Fox went to bed very cross.

Mom came to say good night.

"I wasn't really fooled," said Fox.

"I was just playing along."

"You're so smart," said Mom.